The Cat who Found his Way Home

Michele Coxon

Happy Cat Books

Youstink was a large, fat, dirty cat.

Unlike most cats he did not like washing.

His ginger fur had become very matted and it had turned a muddy brown colour.

It covered old scars and was home to a host of fleas and yesterday's dinner.

Youstink's family was always shouting, "OUT! YOU STINK!" at him, and over the years the name Youstink had stuck to him like the dirt in his fur.

Youstink loved his family (especially Jessica), but he felt sad. He had a feeling in his whiskers that they did not really appreciate all that he did for them.

Youstink sorted out the clean washing and ironing. He tested the food. Too salty?

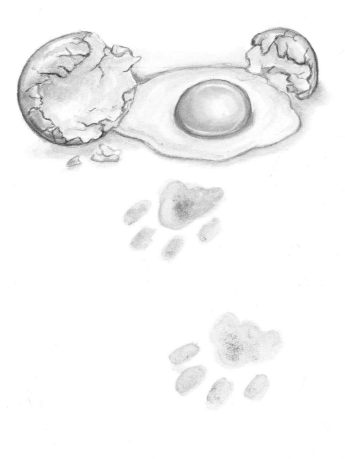

Youstink gave the carpets the right smell and he rearranged the fabric on the sofa with his fine, sharp claws.

Youstink helped the children with their piano lessons.

Youstink went over the children's homework, whatever the weather.

But all these loving cat gestures just brought cries of, "OUT! YOU STINK!"

One busy morning Youstink found an old armchair on the pavement. He decided to climb right inside and have a little catnap.

He was fast asleep when the rag-and-bone man came with his horse and cart and took the armchair away.

He was still fast asleep when the chair was unloaded in the scrap-yard.

Hours later Youstink awoke to the moon and night shadows.

A huge shape loomed out of the dark, snorting fire and smoke.

"Help! A dragon!" howled Youstink.

The dark monster laughed softly and moved closer.

"Please, I came in the armchair and I'm lost. I just want to go home," pleaded Youstink.

"I am only an old horse, but you are two thousand, six hundred and four clip-clops from your street," calculated the horse wisely.

That sounded a very long way away to Youstink.

"I'll never see my family again," Youstink wailed.

"Rubbish!" snorted the horse. "You can use your instinct to find your way home."

Youstink looked all around, but he could not see his instinct anywhere.

The horse explained that most intelligent animals (he paused and looked closely at Youstink) have a feeling inside them.

"It is rather like a compass and it guides you home," he said, and walked off to graze.

Poor Youstink looked up at the star-filled sky and felt himself being pulled towards the moon.

He followed moonbeams all night until he came to a river. He ran along the bank, but there was no bridge and the moon mocked him as it danced on the water.

He leaped on to the moon's reflection, but it shattered into a hundred broken moon drops, each one containing a new moon. Splash!

Youstink came up sneezing and paddled to the opposite bank, where he climbed out looking very wet and bedraggled.

But still Youstink's home and the moon called to him and he ran on through fields of poppies, sweet-smelling herbs and wheat until his paws felt sore and his tail drooped.

Under a wild dogrose Youstink curled himself up into a tight ball of safety and dreams.

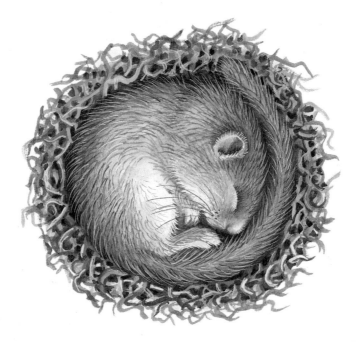

In the dawn of morning the first rays of sun woke Youstink. He forgot his nightmares, stretched out and yawned to the sun.

He felt different. He felt light and clean. His fur, washed in the river, had dried and become soft; it shone gold in the sun. His nose was salmon-pink and, twitching it, he smelt the scent of home.

Youstink walked into town like a lion, listening out for the sounds of his street: church bells, the milkman and barking dogs. Here at last were the familiar smells of the bakery, the butcher's and the fish and chip shop.

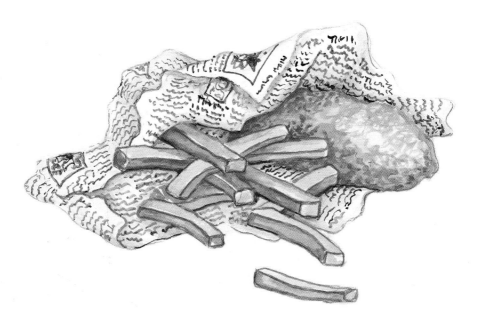

Youstink climbed into his garden. He was home. Jessica saw him first and hugged him until she squeezed nearly all his purrs out of him.

The family hardly recognized Youstink. They were amazed by his beautiful coat and stroked his soft fur. They talked about his golden coat of many colours and how he smelt sweetly of herbs and roses.

"We must give him a new name," they said, and he purred happily until he heard what it was . . .

. . . Petal!